INO NI KANABO: ART OF KAKURE INO

Artwork / Kyle Toorie (Yakusan Kairu)
Book Design / Andrew Norman (Drew Sketch)

Published by Black Artery Studios Inc.
Brooklyn, NY

ISBN-13: 978-0-692-79430-2
ISBN-10: 0-692-79430-1

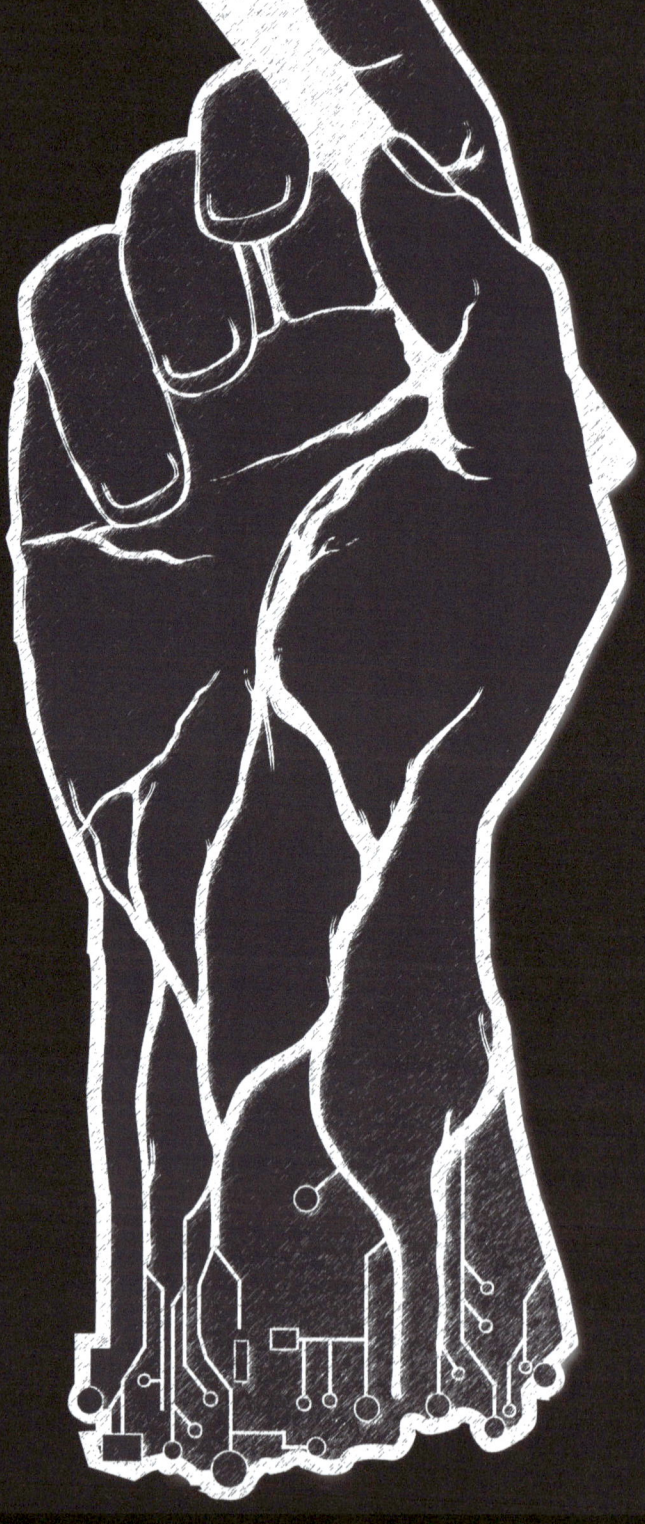

BLACKARTERY ™

*"ART FROM THE HEART; WE BLEED INK FROM THE
VEINS OF 1,000 PIXCELLS"*

BLACK ARTERY STUDIOS

Contact:
blackarterystudios@gmail.com

Website:
www.blackarterystudios.com

Social Media (Instagram):
@yakusan893
@blackarterystudios

INO NI KANABŌ

ART OF KAKURE INO

YAKUSAN KAIRU

INTRODUCTION

FROM THE ARTIST

Hello Reader,

Thank you for purchasing a copy of Ino ni Kanabo: Art of Kakure Ino. I appreciate your interest in my work as this book represents hundreds, perhaps thousands of hours or even years of hard work. The art that graces the pages of this book, are a testament to long hours, sleepless nights and risking write-ups during my day job so that you may have them.

Kakure Ino is a tale of a young Oni named Ino who detests humans and demons alike, while still being a hybrid of both herself. As the last of her kind, she is captured and left with an ultimatum; die in captivity or save Japan and learn of a way to revive her race. Ino must defeat the Four Divine Guardian Beasts who govern the will of nature on earth in order to break into heaven and awaken the sleeping Quilin, the Final Beast who can bring peace and prosperity to the land.

My love for Japanese history and culture shows through my understanding of this work; combined with passion and creativity to bring you, the reader, something you can enjoy. I am also content in my decision to bring forth a female lead to echo the likes of Hayao Miyazaki's films and other known strong female leads like The Major (*Ghost in the Shell*) or Ryuko Matoi (*Kill la Kill*).

Male and female fans alike can enjoy and respect strong female characters, especially the tomboy archetype that is Ino. I can only hope that one day, once the manga is completed, I would be able to attend an anime convention or two and spot a cosplayer dressed as Ino. My dream is not for me alone, but one to be shared with my fans as we are all lovers of art and creativity; manga, anime, or otherwise.

Once more, thank you for buying my book. It is the first and most definitely not the last of a long line of Black Artery Artbooks. Drew Sketch and I are proud of the amount of work we go through when putting this kind of a project together. It is a culmination of our teamwork and we hope that you are able to enjoy every inch of this product; inside and out.

Remember, I am nothing special without you. So please, without further delay, enjoy Ino ni Kanabo.

Kairu "Yakusan" Toorie
Black Artery Studios

About The Artist

Yakusan Kairu (Kyle Toorie) is an African American illustrator of West Indian/Caribbean descent, born and raised in New York. Since the age of 5, Yakusan has been doodling on paper and drawing forms competently by age 7. Now 28 years old; Yakusan has been consistently creating various works for over 20 years using a variety of subject matter and mediums. He received formal education in portraiture and fine arts study and has been able to combine it with his childhood love for manga to create new ideas and designs that carry weight to them. Along with an extensive and genuine interest in Japanese history this allowed him to conceive Kakure Ino and develop it.

Yakusan has brought many ideas to life; visually as an independent character designer for several independent writers, including long time friend and business partner Drew Sketch. Together, the two have founded Black Artery Studios; a freelance company dealing with commission based works and artbook publication to help others live out their vision on paper.

Yakusan carries on as an aspiring manga creator and comic book artist. He remains dedicated to telling stories regardless of the format or subject matter. Whether through graphic novels, artbooks, or single illustrations, the goal is to paint a picture of 1,000 words; mirroring the years of influences and inspirations that have collected for nearly 30 years. Yakusan's primary mediums are mechanical pencils, pens, and alcohol based markers combined with color pencils. His style ranges from **traditional Japanese manga** to life-like realism, only recently finding the perfect balance after many years of practice. Other mediums include watercolor paint and in a pinch; Photoshop.

Supported with a small fan base and several projects in the works, Yakusan continues to inspire others and is a source of motivation and advice for his peers. Always there to lend a helping hand, he continues to give lessons in art whenever possible. His own influences are manga artists Tetsuo Hara (*Fist of the North Star*), Kentaro Miura (*Berserk*), and Takehiko Inoue (*Vagabond*) as well as Leonardo da Vinci for his precision and accuracy and lastly, Sandro Botticelli for his composition and use of one point perspective. On occasion, Yakusan moonlights as a Nude Muse pin-up artist in his spare time to keep his anatomical skills sharp.

Yakusan conceived his nickname from working late shifts at a casino. Yakusan or "8-9-3" is a losing hand in a Japanese card game. This was chosen to display the irony and struggles of everyday life that he witnessed at the casino. And the name has remained ever since.

鬼に金棒

oni-ni-kanabō
(oni with an ironclub)

To be invincible or unbeatable.
or "*strong beyond strong*"

ABOUT THE TITLE

The word "oni" is sometimes speculated to be derived from on, the on'yomi reading of a character meaning to hide or conceal, as oni were originally invisible spirits or gods which caused disasters, disease, and other unpleasant occurrences. These nebulous beings could also take on a variety of forms to deceive and often devour humans.

The invisible oni eventually became anthropomorphized and took on its modern, ogre-like form, partly via syncretism with creatures imported by Buddhism, such as the Indian rakshasa and yaksha.

The title was called such due to the constant use of "hidden" creatures, including Ino herself. Hiding from violent humans, hiding from her responsibility as a potential savior, the Four Guardians Beasts are hidden away and Ino must find them. Hidden truths and lies, Hidden power, etc.

Ironically, in stark contrast with the "Oni ni Kanabo" quote, it implies that Oni should never hide, because they are strong and that in itself speaks of the transformation Ino undergoes from a hated and feared demon, to a revered savior.

Kakurenbo - Hide and Seek

Kakure - To be hidden

ONI - INO

INO

Ino is my daughter and as such my first true original character. I have developed and revised her design over and over again. It took years to finally settle on what I believed to be a strong design befitting of a main character and hero.

INO
AGE: 17

鬼に金棒
鬼に金棒

Unmarked
Necklace

Leather/cloth
Legging
(Given from dead)
Paige Boy

— Ino the Oni —(BARE)
CHARACTER DESIGN SHEET
1st ARC

5'1"

Body covered in scars

Hands & Feet on large side and clawed

Slim Petite Figure

Secondary original drawing of Ino when she was still a male character.

Thick Wild Hair
Rough Thick Brows
Almond Eyes
Wide Mouth
Slender Face
Small Fangs
Large Ears
Small Nose

INO FACE TEMPLATE

KAKURE INO

KAKURE INO
COVER THUMB 1

Arrogant
painful
face.

Reference
Nuc head
(More dead stare)
(less blood/gore)

Show more of club

Title

'Kanabō Midori'

Jade Club
Made from
emerald found
in China

Old Scroll
Meant to
read:
(strongest
in the Heavens)

INO

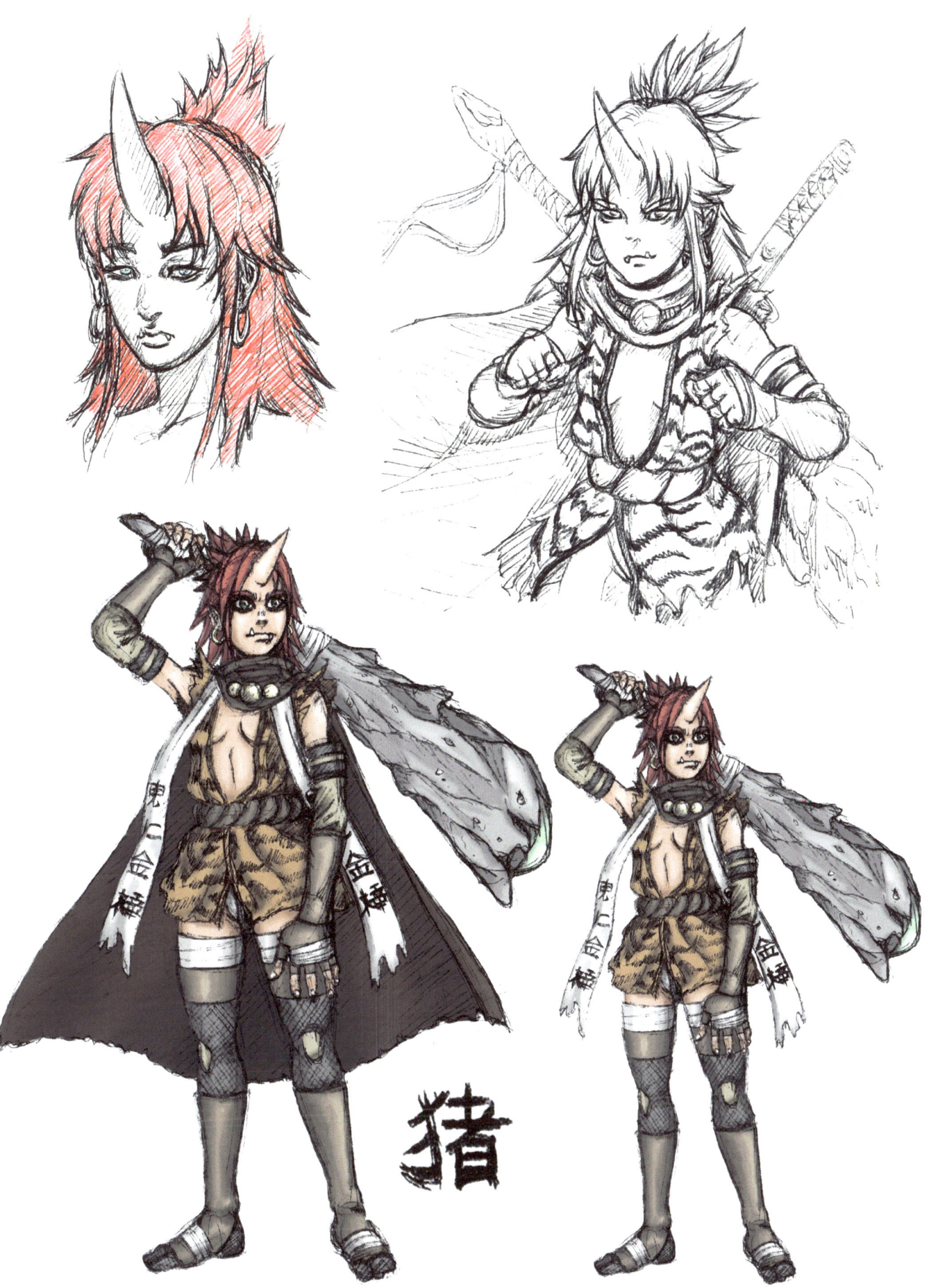

猪

*By Unknown Artist
(Uncredited)

*By ShinrinYoru
(Real Name Unknown)

SENGO

Although I am most proud of Ino, my favorite character design happens to be Sengo. Cut from the same cloth as Ino, as a demon what sets Sengo apart is the silence of her strength and apparent calmness of character. Her design is mature and strong.

正宗千子

SENGO
AGE: 300

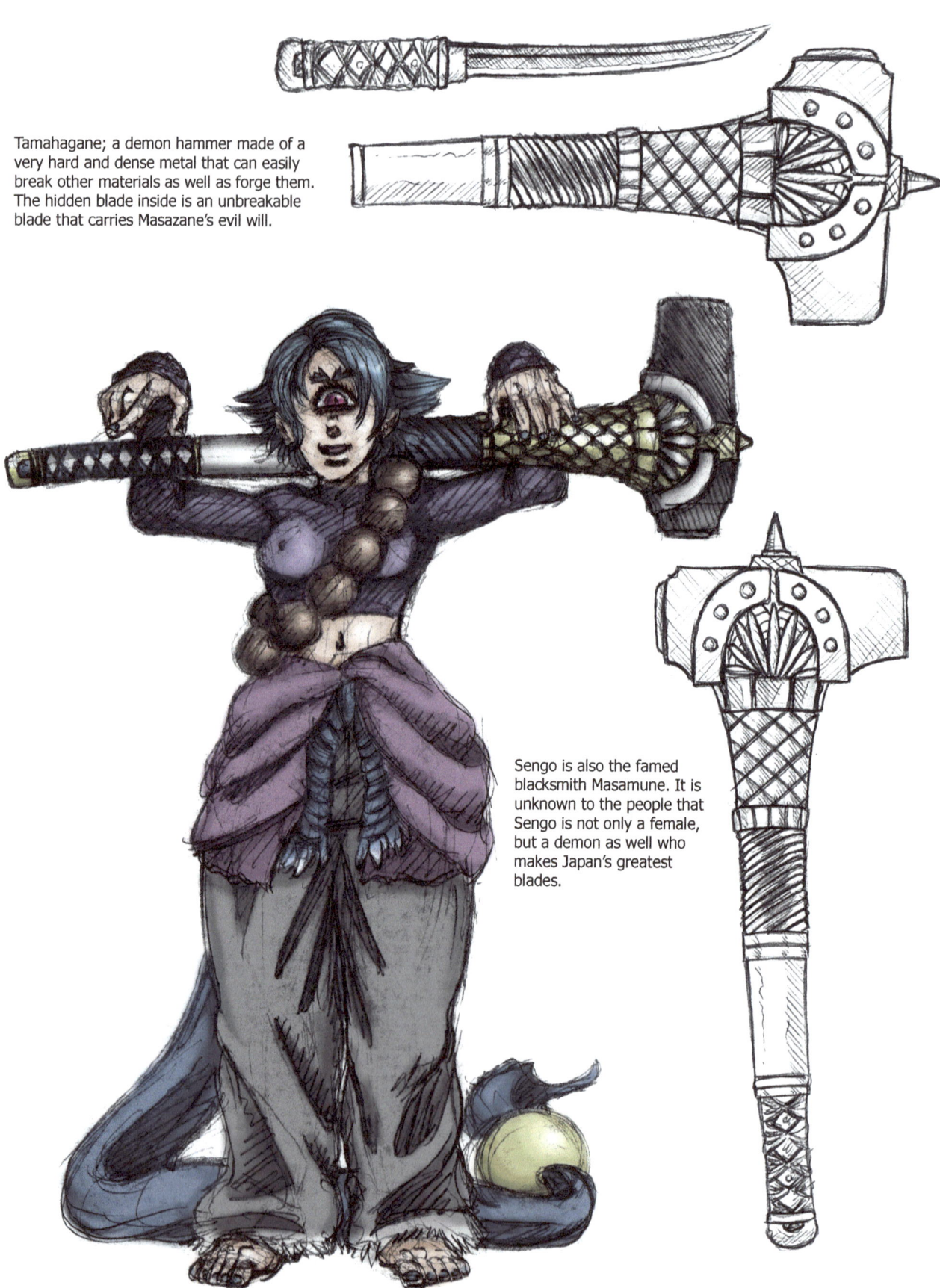

Tamahagane; a demon hammer made of a very hard and dense metal that can easily break other materials as well as forge them. The hidden blade inside is an unbreakable blade that carries Masazane's evil will.

Sengo is also the famed blacksmith Masamune. It is unknown to the people that Sengo is not only a female, but a demon as well who makes Japan's greatest blades.

MASAMUNE
SENGO

"Cold"
Color
Scheme

Needs
Somethin'

Meryl
Hairstyle

Buddhist
Beads

Torn
top

Painted
toenails
&
fingernails

Braided
tailed Obi
w/ Bead

Born to a
HITOTSUME
MOTHER &
FATHER
(ONE EYE)

Deads
from Tang Dynasty
chine (Buddhist)

"Tamahagane"
A Godly HAMMER
that can destroy
and Forge any
Material

AGE: 300 YEARS
HGT: 4'9
WHT: 100lbs
ORGN: CHANG'AN, CHINA
WPN: SMITHING HAMMER
RACE: HITOTSUME YOKAI

SENGO

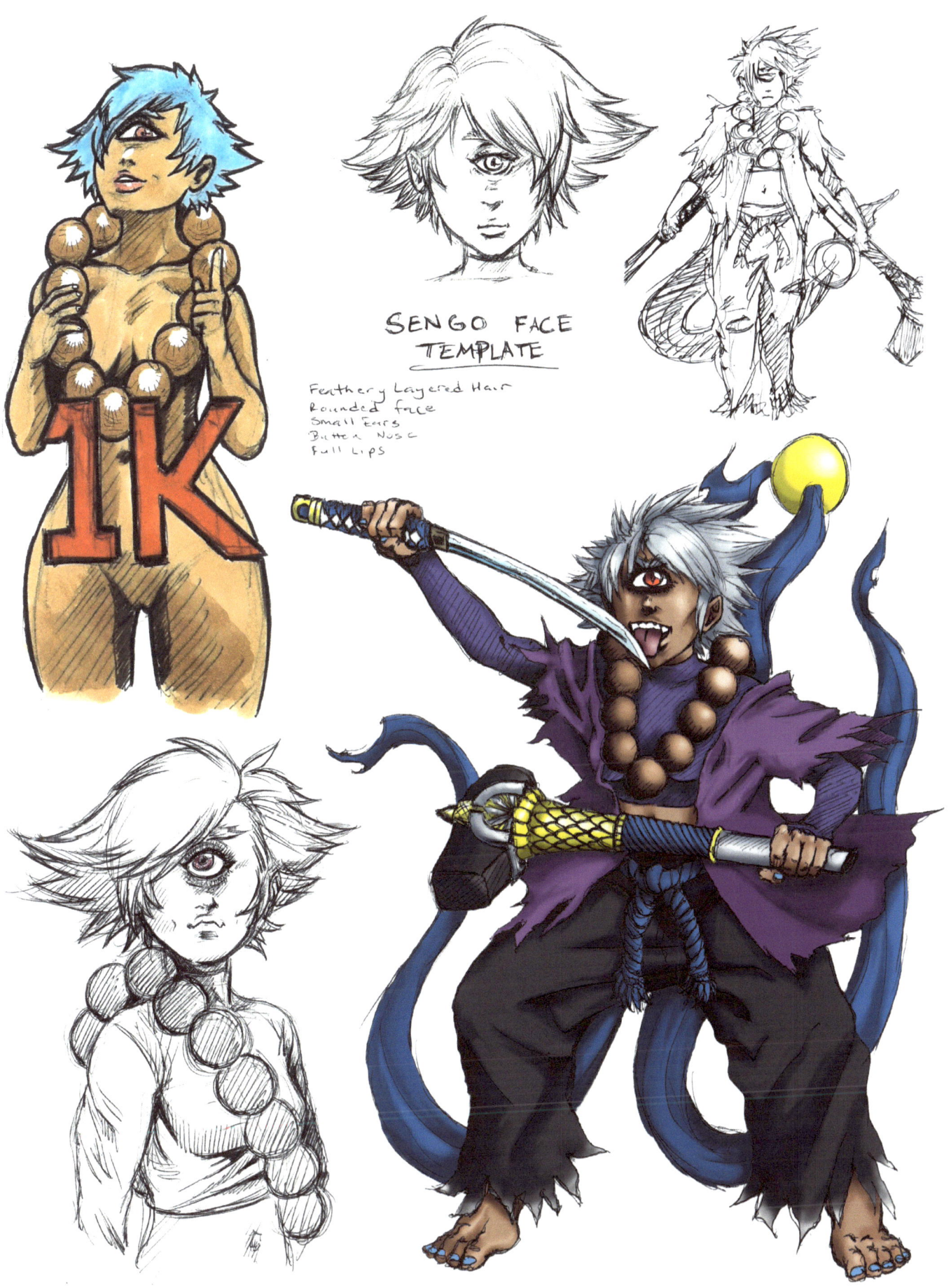

SENGO FACE
TEMPLATE

Feathery Layered Hair
Rounded face
Small Ears
Button Nose
Full Lips

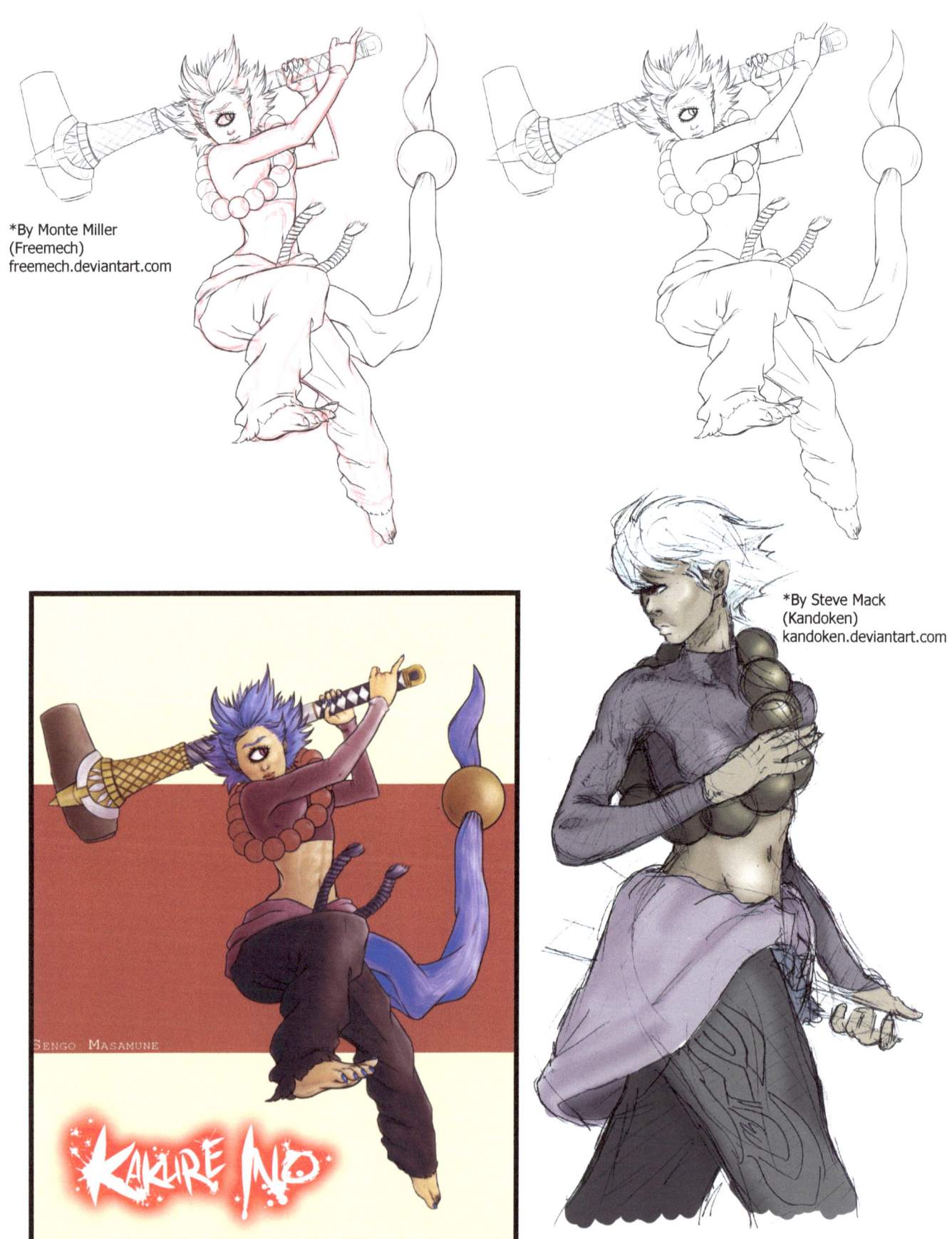

*By Monte Miller
(Freemech)
freemech.deviantart.com

*By Steve Mack
(Kandoken)
kandoken.deviantart.com

SENGO MASAMUNE

KAKURE INO

Compared size comparison model

KAKURE_INO

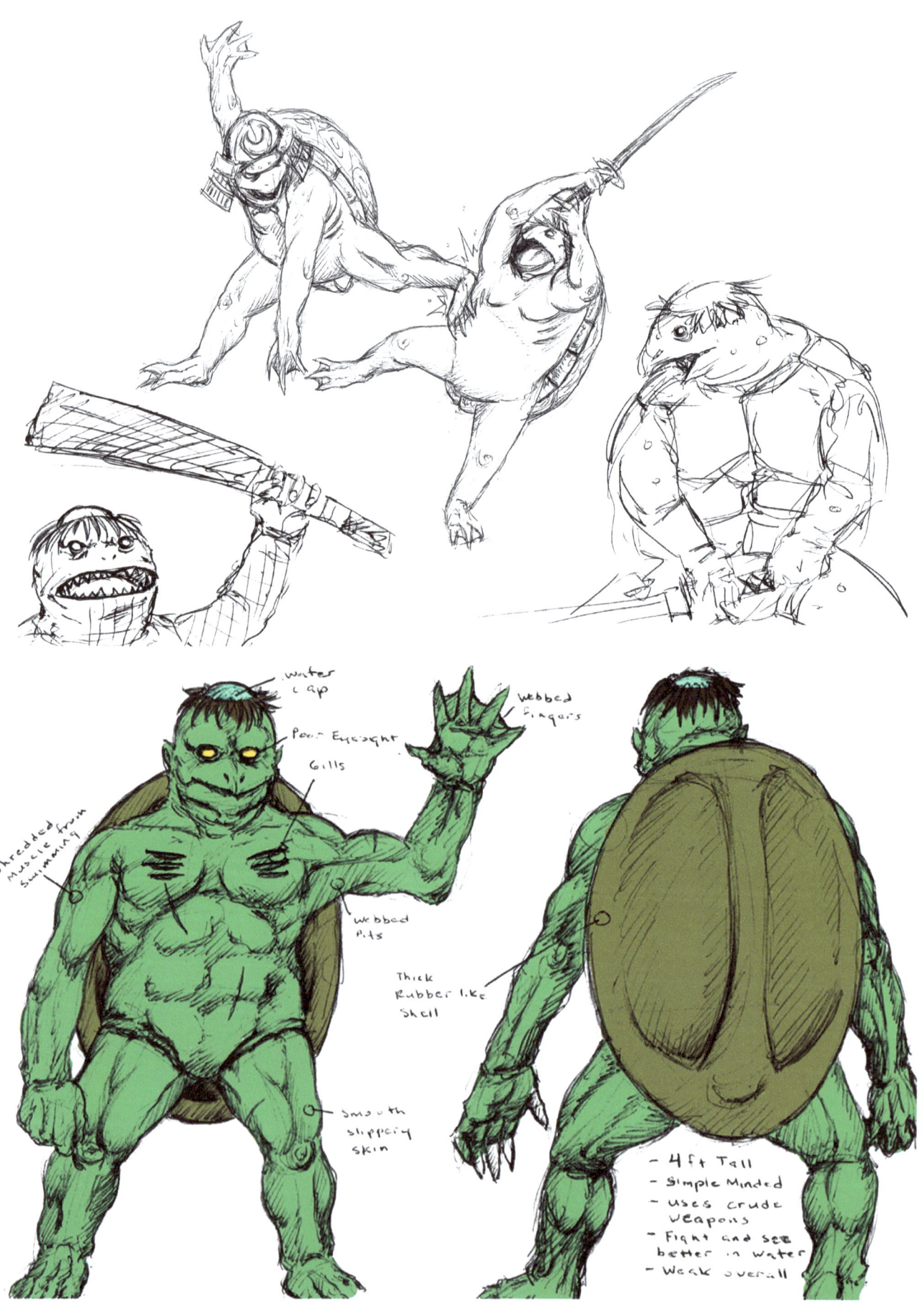

water cap

Poor Eyesight

Gills

Shredded from Muscle from Swimming

Webbed Fingers

Webbed Pits

Thick Rubber like Shell

Smooth slippery Skin

- 4ft Tall
- Simple Minded
- uses crude weapons
- Fight and see better in water
- Weak overall

Kappa Boss #1

Harder more durable shell

Cares for Kappa + Boss #2

Blood Rusted Saw Blade

Always stays close to like sumo

Kappa Boss #2

Taller of the two
Better fighter
Always kneeling when fighting humans

Fat Kappa Boss

Skinny Kappa Boss

WHY A FEMALE LEAD?

With the consistent influx of manga and anime into mainstream western life, we have all been in one way or another influenced by some creation of Japanese origin, be it *Dragon Ball Z* or *Godzilla*. We also live in a patriarchal society where the male still takes precedence in the minds of many although women have been able to experience more freedom through their voice and struggles. Women have a voice, a powerful one, and that includes fans of videogames, manga, anime etc and often times, man will like what the lady likes. With our women holding such power it is imperative that they too receive proper representation in the light that they deserve.

The female characters I choose to draw represent power, sometimes in a masculine way or in a robust way that results in a myriad of interesting designs. From elegant to rough, nearly all of my female characters are either fighting women or for the most part, not helpless.

As a man who was raised by his mother, aunt, and grandmother, the female holds a special place in my work and my heart. Not as a piece of meat, but as an object of beauty and admiration and I say this in earnest out of respect, without a pedestal. They hold marketing and buying power and are the leading consumer and admirers of great art.

Although I did not consider why I chose a female character for this project back in 2004 (Ino originally was a male Oni), I was able to reaffirm my decision as I continually witness the hardships and struggles of women in our world. The pain of giving birth, the struggle of raising a child alone, the abuse, the lack of opportunity, the doubting by men and the sexual assumption and advances.

These are only some issues to name a few but in all of these situations, women call for strength and power. The ability to overcome. Ino is my answer to that call. The physical representation of power in a world that shuns her kind. Like Ino, our women have had to prove themselves time and time again under harsh and unfairly impossible conditions.I can only hope that this will be one of many opportunites I receive to uplift them with a story of triumph.

*By Steve Mack
(Kandoken)
kandoken.deviantart.com

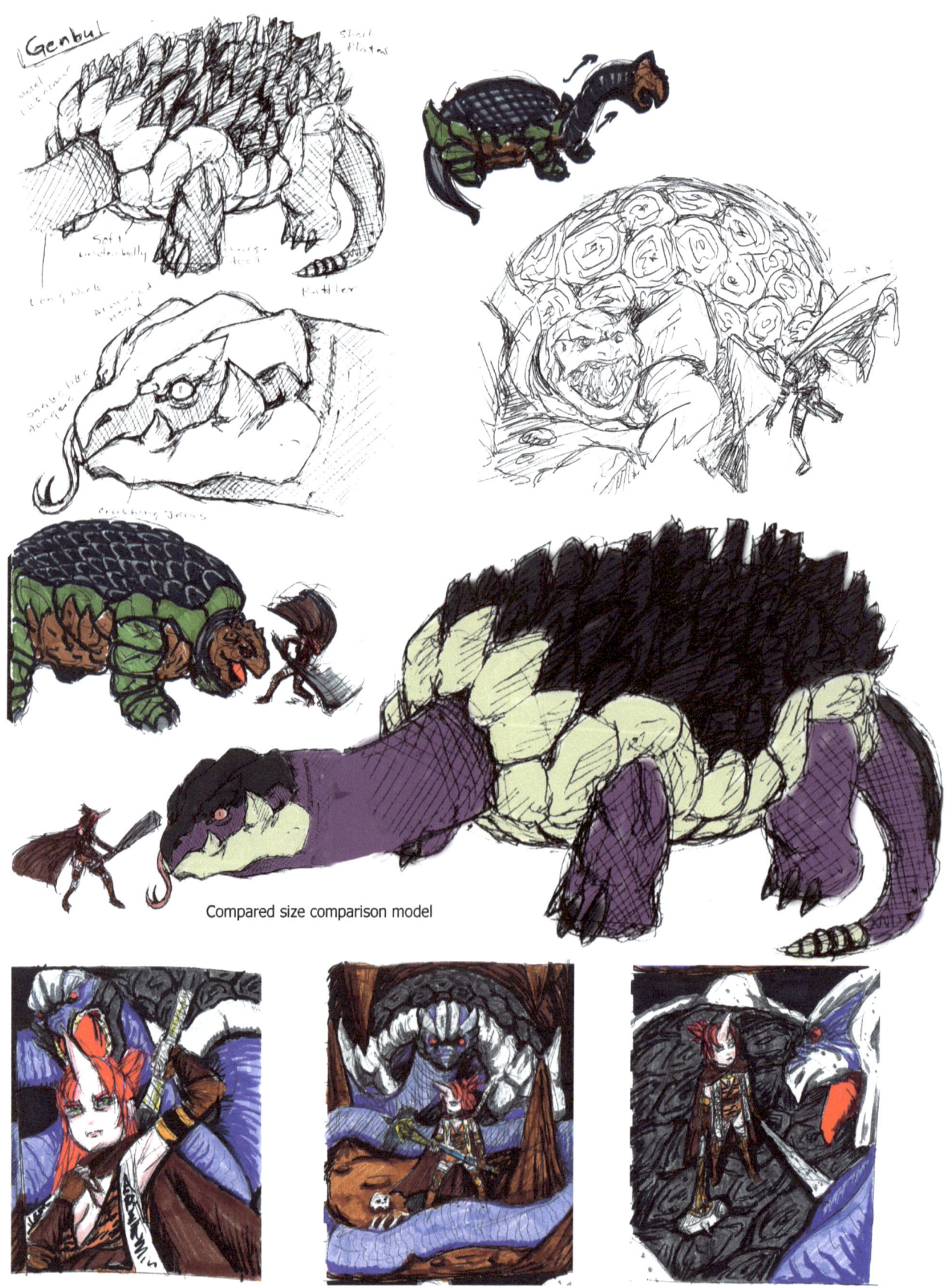

Genbu

Compared size comparison model

BENKEI

Benkei is my anchor, the archetypical strong male character that people are used to relying on. His strength and intimidating demeanor should automatically be reminiscent of your heroic tough guy.

弁慶

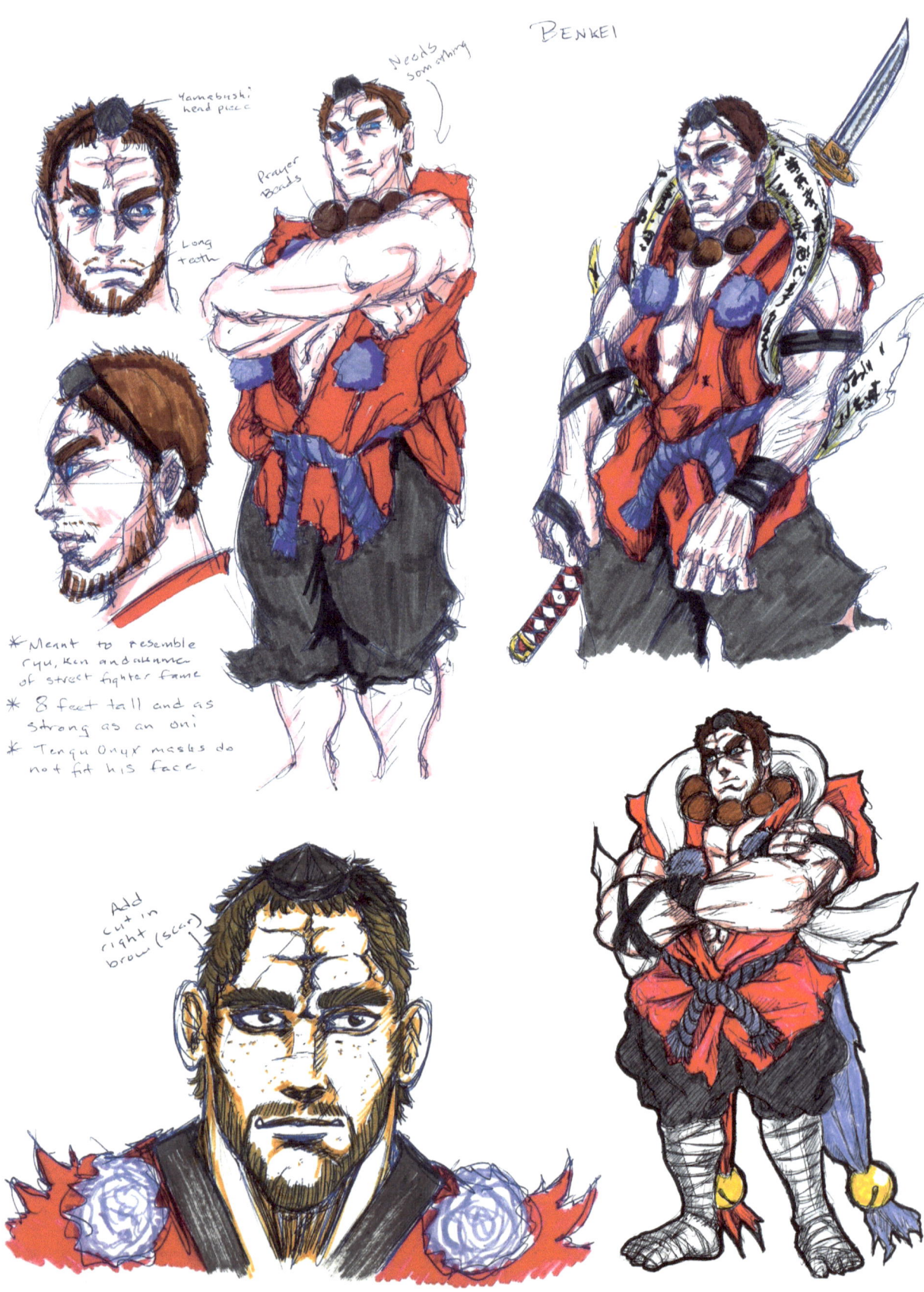

Yamebushi head piece

Needs something

Prayer Beads

Long teeth

BENKEI

* Meant to resemble ryu, ken and akuma of street fighter fame
* 8 feet tall and as strong as an oni
* Tengu Onyx masks do not fit his face.

Add cut in right brow (scar)

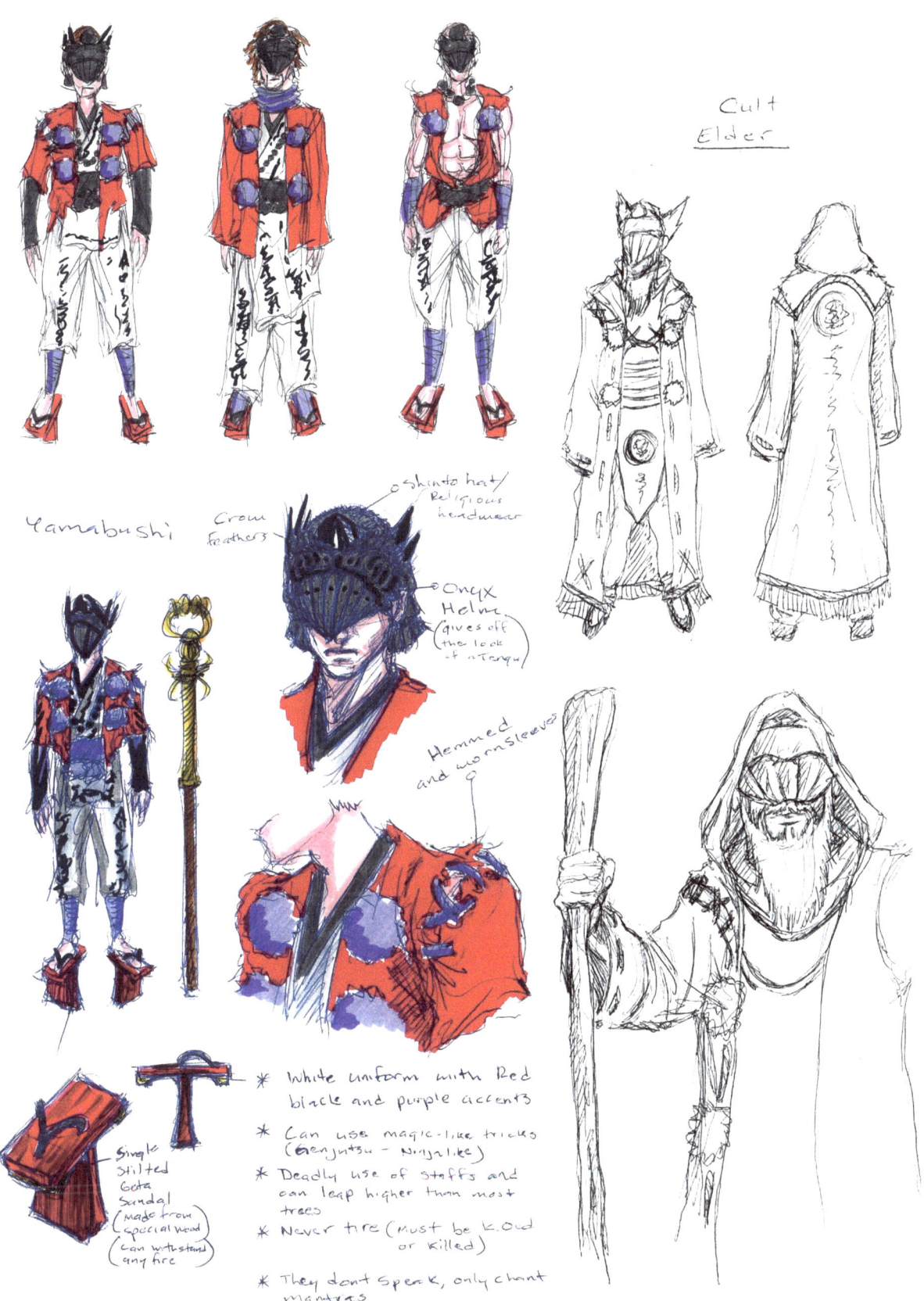

Cult Elder

Yamabushi

Crow Feathers

Shinto hat / Religious headwear

Onyx Helm (gives off the look of a Tengu)

Hemmed and worn sleeves

Single Stilted Geta Sandal (made from special wood) (can withstand any fire)

* White uniform with Red black and purple accents
* Can use magic-like tricks (Genjutsu – Ninja like)
* Deadly use of staffs and can leap higher than most trees
* Never tire (must be K.Od or killed)
* They don't speak, only chant mantras

*By Jiro
(Karnivor Studios)
karnxjiro.deviantart.com

*By Jiro
(Karnivor Studios)
karnxjiro.deviantart.com

Braided Peacock tail w sun ring dream catcher attachment.

Suzaku

Armored Head

Armored Scaled Leg and Talon!

Razor sharp Beak

Compared size comparison model

*By Steve Mack
(Kandoken)
kandoken.deviantart.com

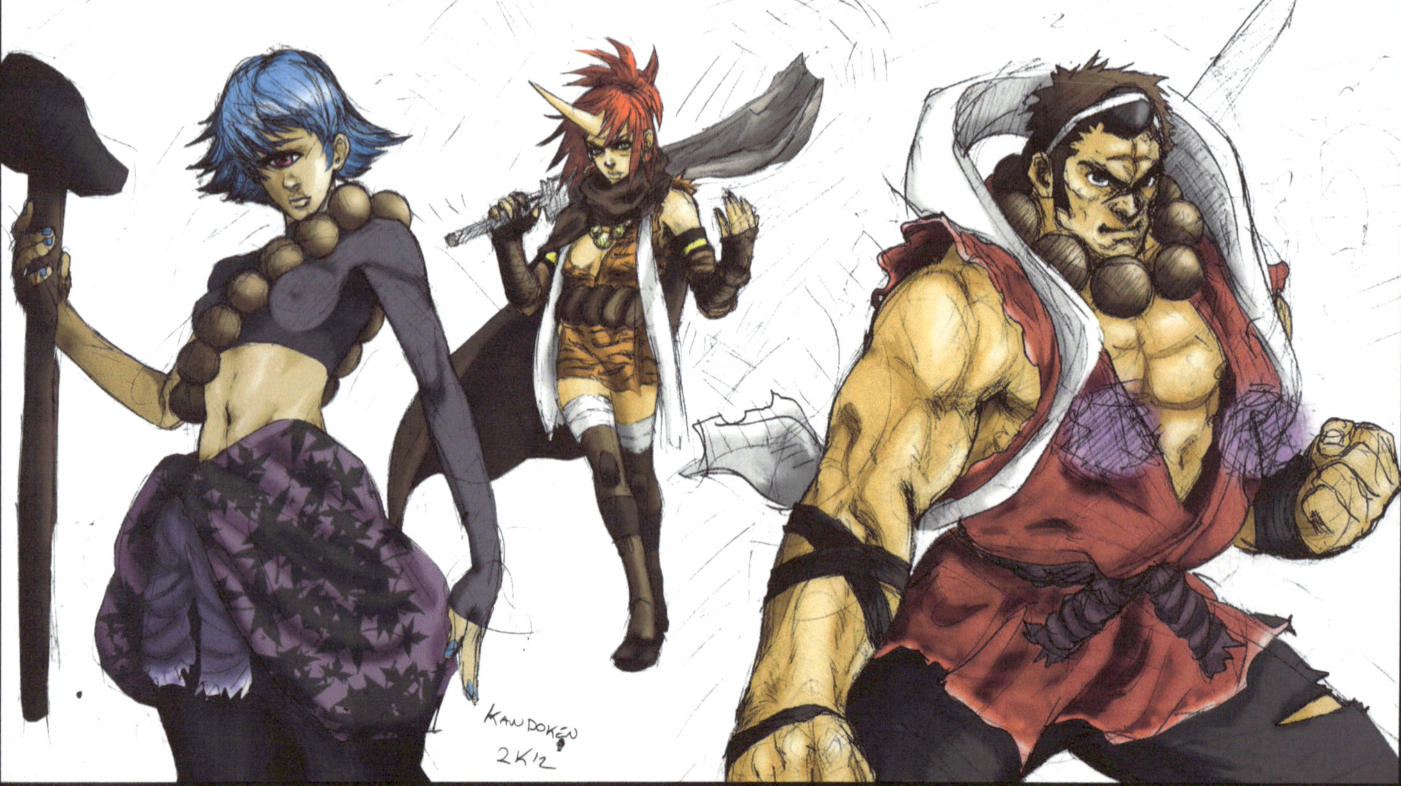

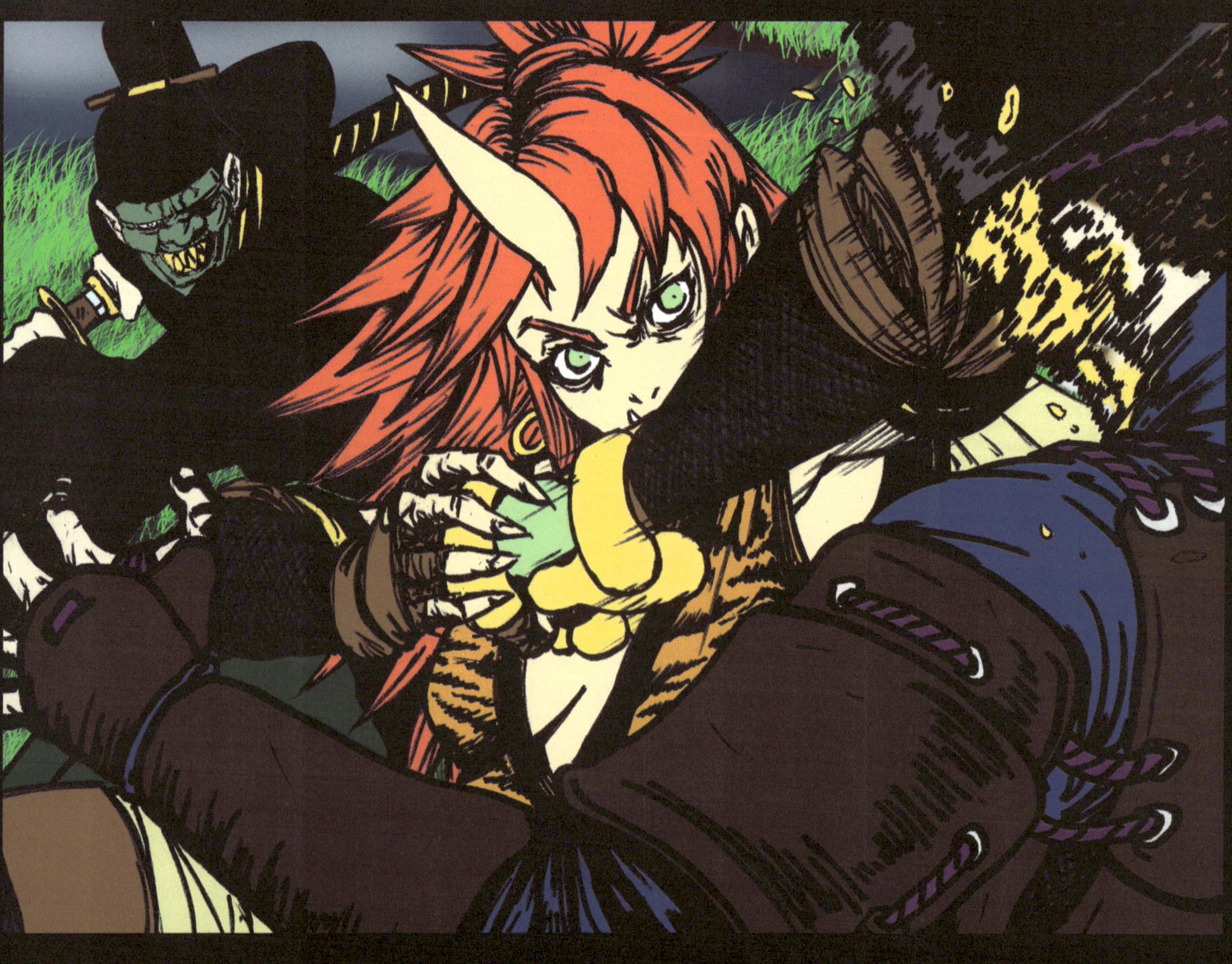

NOTES ON OUTFIT DESIGNS FOR CHARACTERS

This has always been a fun aspect of my creative and imaginative works. Characters like Yoshitsune and Benkei were historical figures and have already had many renditions of them created by others. With so many existing variations its sometimes difficult to be unique in the overall design. More often than not, characters from all works are most often recognizable by what they wear as much as their hair or face.

While Drew Sketch took interest in fashion design, I myself never really considered myself a "costume designer" in that respect. Ironically, in this particular book is where I've had to flex my fashion muscle the most as some of the character outfits started off too generic. Also, the painstaking detail put into the armor of Yoshimitsu was hard on my hand. For the most part I was familiar with traditional Japanese clothing and samurai wear, but to make it intriguing yet simple was the goal and I think I've succeeded in finding a visual balance in the ensembles.

Color schemes also play a huge part in indentifying the personality of the characters. For example; Ino is warm and orange for her fiery nature. Yoshitsune is blue and calm, a very soft spoken individual. Purple for Sengo, as she is mainly laid back but exhibits a warmness to her cool side. And Benkei is red for his violent and brutish ways, like Ino a hot head. Color coordination is very important for not just setting characters apart but for auto suggestion, what your brain automatically tells you based on how a color makes you feel.

The things that have been most helpful to my outfit designs are eccentric characters from video games such as Dynasty Warriors or Final Fantasy (Nomura designs) which push the envelope of conventional clothing and armor. When unsure about what to try or when suffering from artist block on outfits, look through a Paris fashion show, research old and new fashion trends, foreign looks and ancient clothing. Put it in a pot and mix it, you'd be surprised with the results in your sketch book.

Personally the most difficult costume design was actually Raikobo; the purple Tengu god. Even now I dont believe im geniunely satisfied with his outfit design as I am with Ino or Benkei's.

"Costume design allows you to do a different type of research and create characters, whereas in fashion, you create an image and clothing for the masses."

-Colleen Atwood

Compared size comparison model

*By Julia
(Teralilac)
teralilac.deviantart.com

YOSHITSUNE

It is always rough to have a female lead and female support surrounded by rugged male characters without having someone fit for the female fans. Yoshitsune is also a gift to female fans as the young handsome male-type they could swoon over. Devilish looks and a dangerous smile accompany his two swords.

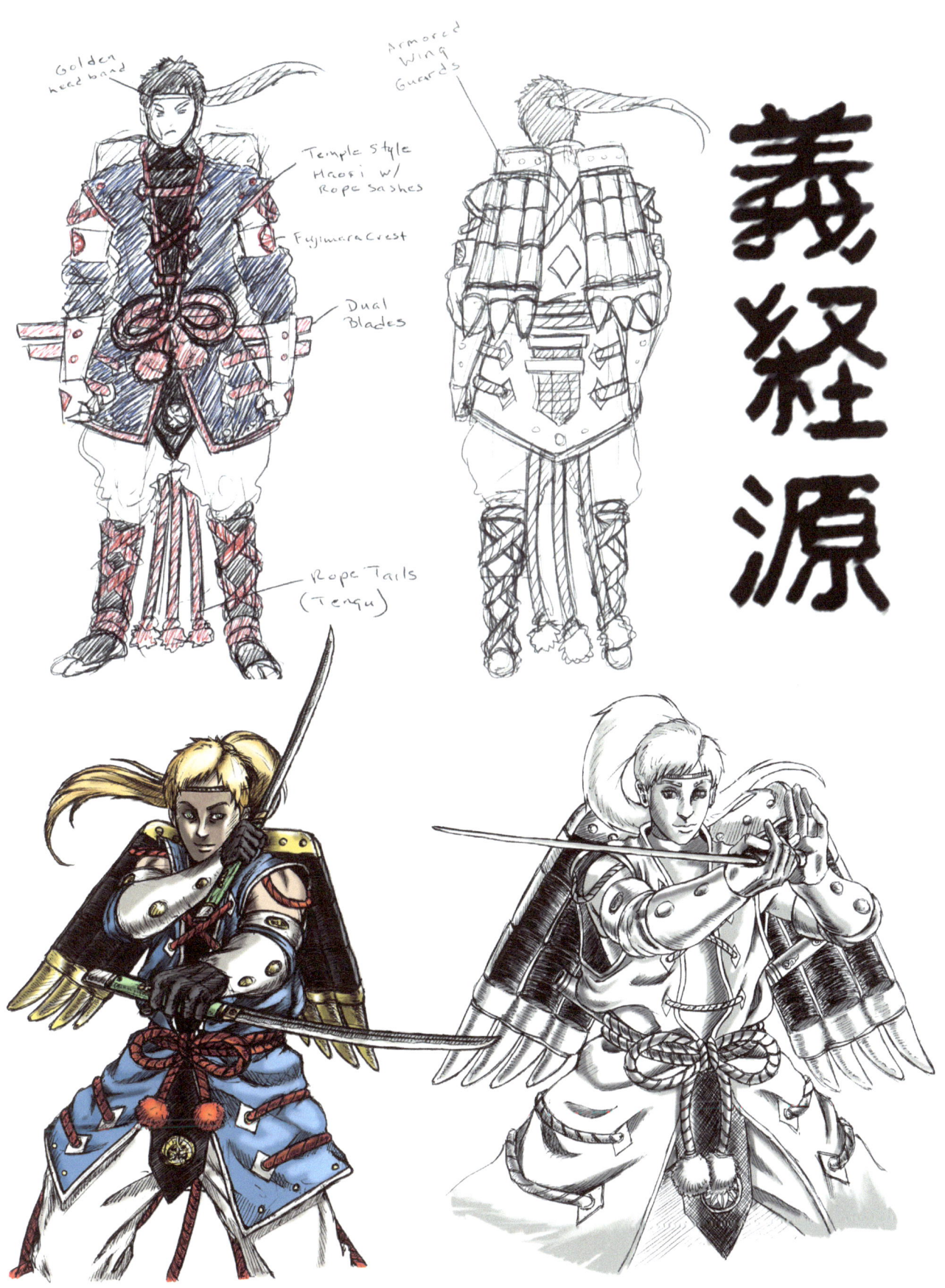

Golden head band

Armored Wing Guards

Temple Style Haori w/ Rope Sashes

Fujimura Crest

Dual Blades

Rope Tails (Tengu)

義経源

KURO'S
HEADDRESS

KURO (YOSHITSUNE)

- Very Young About 17
  years old.

  - Soft features
    almost feminine

- Two sword style based
  on technique & agility

*By Giovana Leandro da Silva Basilio

源の天狗

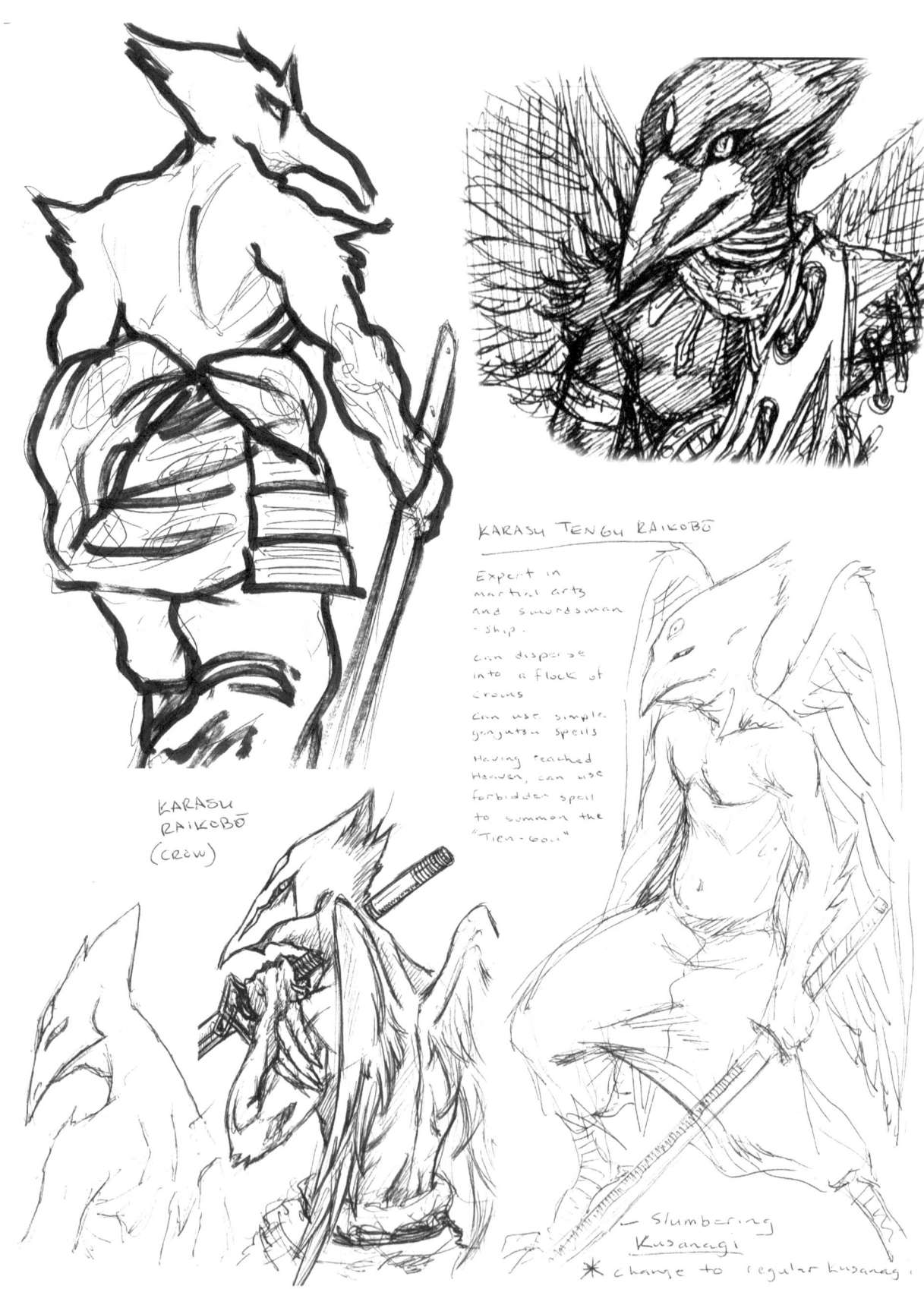

KARASU TENGU RAIKOBŌ

Expert in
martial arts
and swordsman
-ship.

Can disperse
into a flock of
crows

Can use simple
genjutsu spells

Having reached
Heaven, can use
forbidden spell
to summon the
"Tien-Gou"

KARASU
RAIKOBŌ
(CROW)

— Slumbering
Kusanagi
* change to regular kusanagi.

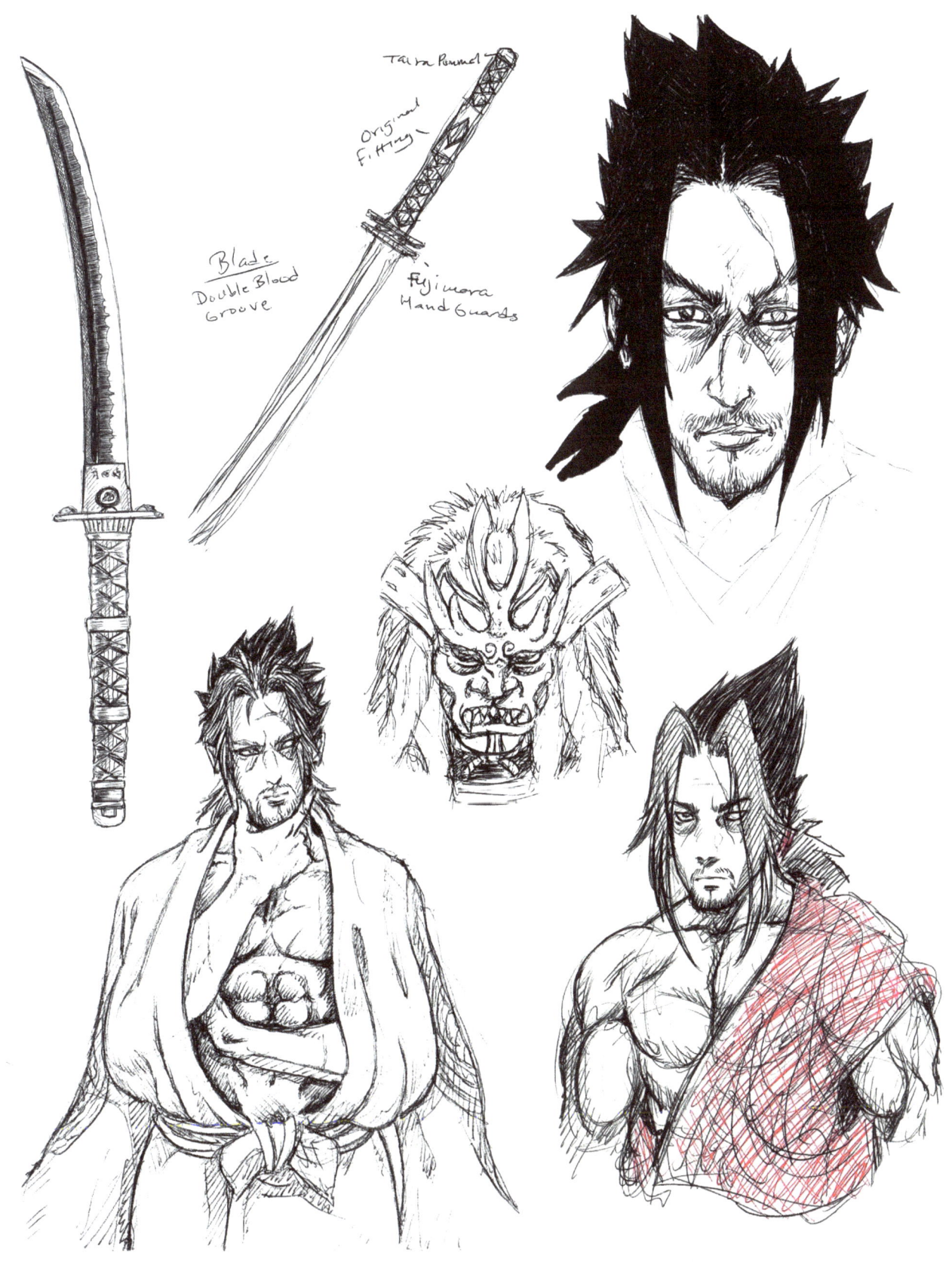

Taira Pommel

Original Fitting

Blade:
Double Blood
Groove

Fujimora
Hand Guards

Guard
Eyepatch

Magatama

Yoshimitsu
Shinnosuke

Fujiwara
crest

Golden
Armor

O-Kabuto

O-yoroi
Armor

TAIRA NO YOSHIMITSU

Fujiwara Soldiers (Armor)

Spear Infantry

Swordsman
* Elites wear thicker armor
+ Kabuto

Archer

Chinese style armor

court headwear
clay mask

Lon Tac

Royal

Spear

Archer

Demon Face

Nasu no Yoichi

MINAMOTO

Akai Kodomo
(Red children)

平清盛

TAIRA

Inari is an Ainu and I wanted to show the features of that kind of culture through her clothing. The trinkets and furs as well as the dagger show a cultural contrast to the more noble Japanese of the time.

Rain woman
- Thin wet black hair
- Eyes disolved from crying
- Zombie like, shuffles along wailing and looking around
- Pasty white skin & soaked clothes

Rain child
- Wet black hair
- Pasty white skin
- Lively white glowing eyes
- Carries around an umbrella
- Mischievous & playful
- Emits a creepy giggle or chuckle
- Loves hide & seek

Wanyudo

Feeding Form

(Snow White)

Hair Parted to hide eye

Bell choker

Beauty Form

Masked
Shadow

THOUGHTS ON YOKAI (MONSTER DESIGN)

Without a doubt, I have to say this is the most fun and creative part of the work. The Yokai (Japanese Demons) come in all types from humanoid creatures, large beasts, and ghastly apparitions and yet, unlike normal character designs, this is where I get to implement my craziest ideas. Anything is literally possible when creating a monster and nothing is off limits.

My favorite creatures to design are the run of the mill cannon fodder; the enemies that the character faces the most and are always ripe for a beating. The lil guy below is one such example of the Imp, riding off of my own Oni designs. Deviating from the massive and bulky Oni, I questioned how could I make it fearsome and yet able to be taken down by the same humans that it hunts. It would be more primitive than most, attacking out of instinctual fear instead of reason. Its hunched form and old man features add a sort of awkward frailty to it although it is stronger than a human. Finding a believable balance while maintaining simplicity and directness was key.

One method that helps when creating a monster from scratch is writing down descriptive ideas on one side of a sheet. "Big hairy ears, wide frightened eyes, large wide nose, pointed dome skull, human bones, potbelly", are all keywords to to feed your imagination whilst maintaining limitations of what you are aiming to create.

Naturally, most things have been done before, or rather similar designs but even the costume design on a creature if any, can set them apart. I can name inspirations such as the Bokoblin of Zelda: Skyward Sword or the Jonin Red of Tenchu: Wrath of Heaven, that I did not directly use but recall with memory and experience.

Essentially, it is important to have fun. Enjoy your wild ideas when going in on monsters and make them shine when going up against the hero. Sometimes human vs human battles can get a little redundant or outright boring in a fantasy setting and the right kind of freak will spice things up.

Any living animal at its base, even humans can become Yokai or demons by adding, mixing and matching random parts together.

Onyx w/
Gold Lining

FEMALE
WATER IMP

MALE
WATER IMP

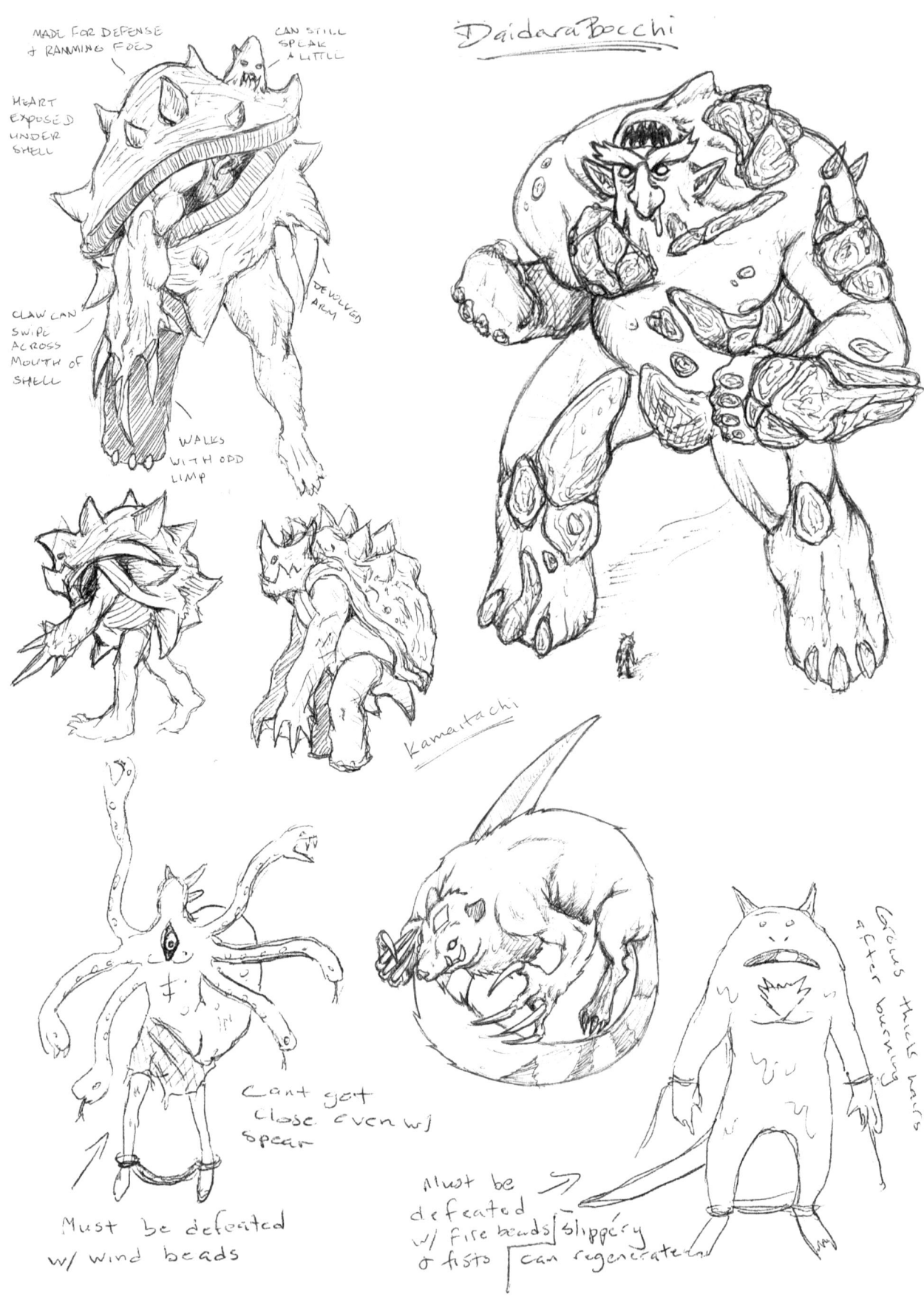

MADE FOR DEFENSE + RAMMING FOES

CAN STILL SPEAK A LITTLE

Daidarabocchi

HEART EXPOSED UNDER SHELL

CLAW CAN SWIPE ACROSS MOUTH OF SHELL

DEVOLVED ARM

WALKS WITH ODD LIMP

Kamaitachi

Can't get close even w/ spear

Must be defeated w/ wind beads

Must be defeated w/ fire beads ⃗ & fists

slippery ⌐ can regenerate

Grows thick hairs after burning

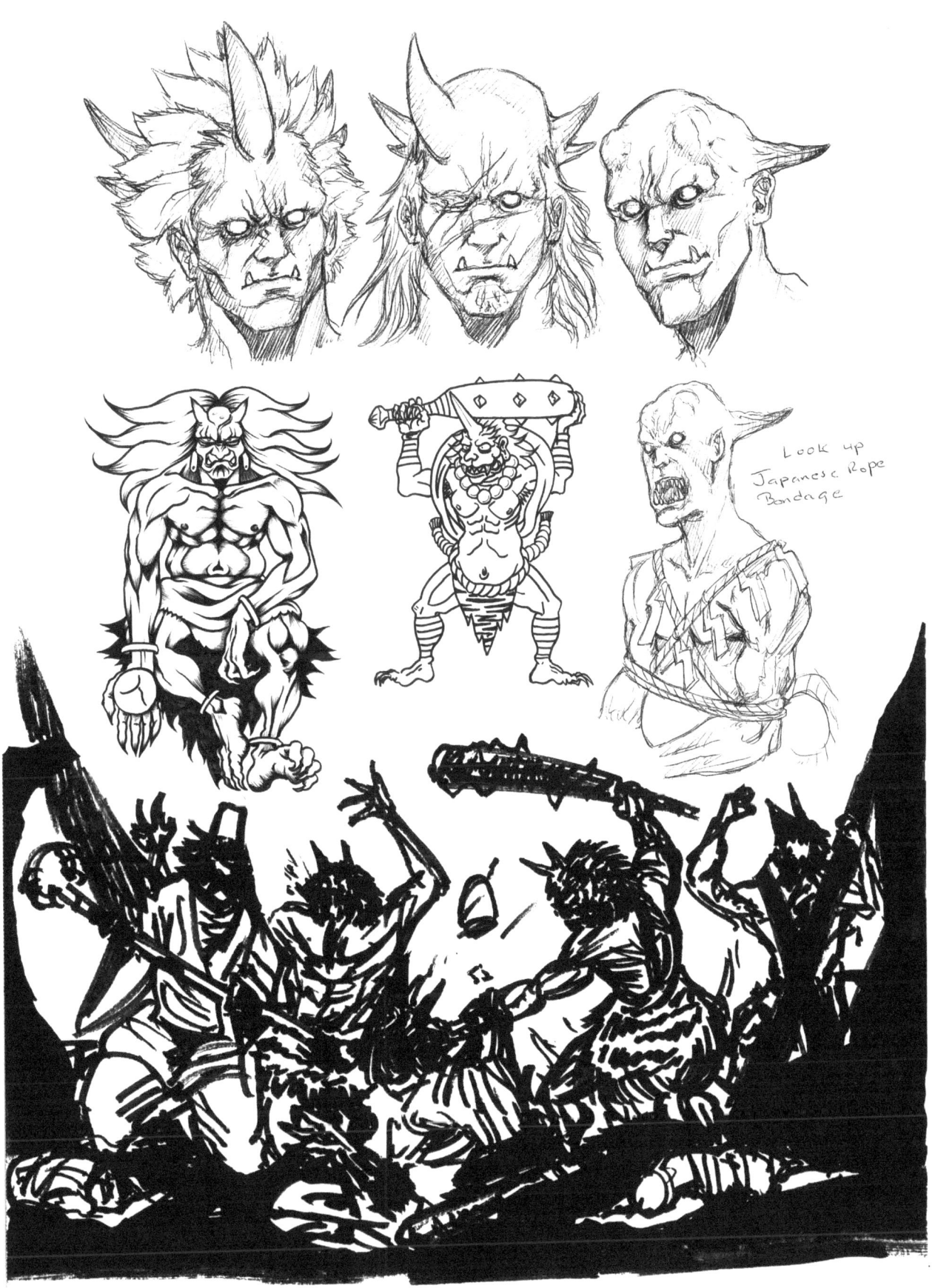

Look up
Japanese Rope
Bondage

Doji
Thumb

DOJI

SHUTEN DOJI

More
Muscular
yet
slightly
deformed

discolored
burn
scars +
self tested
cutter

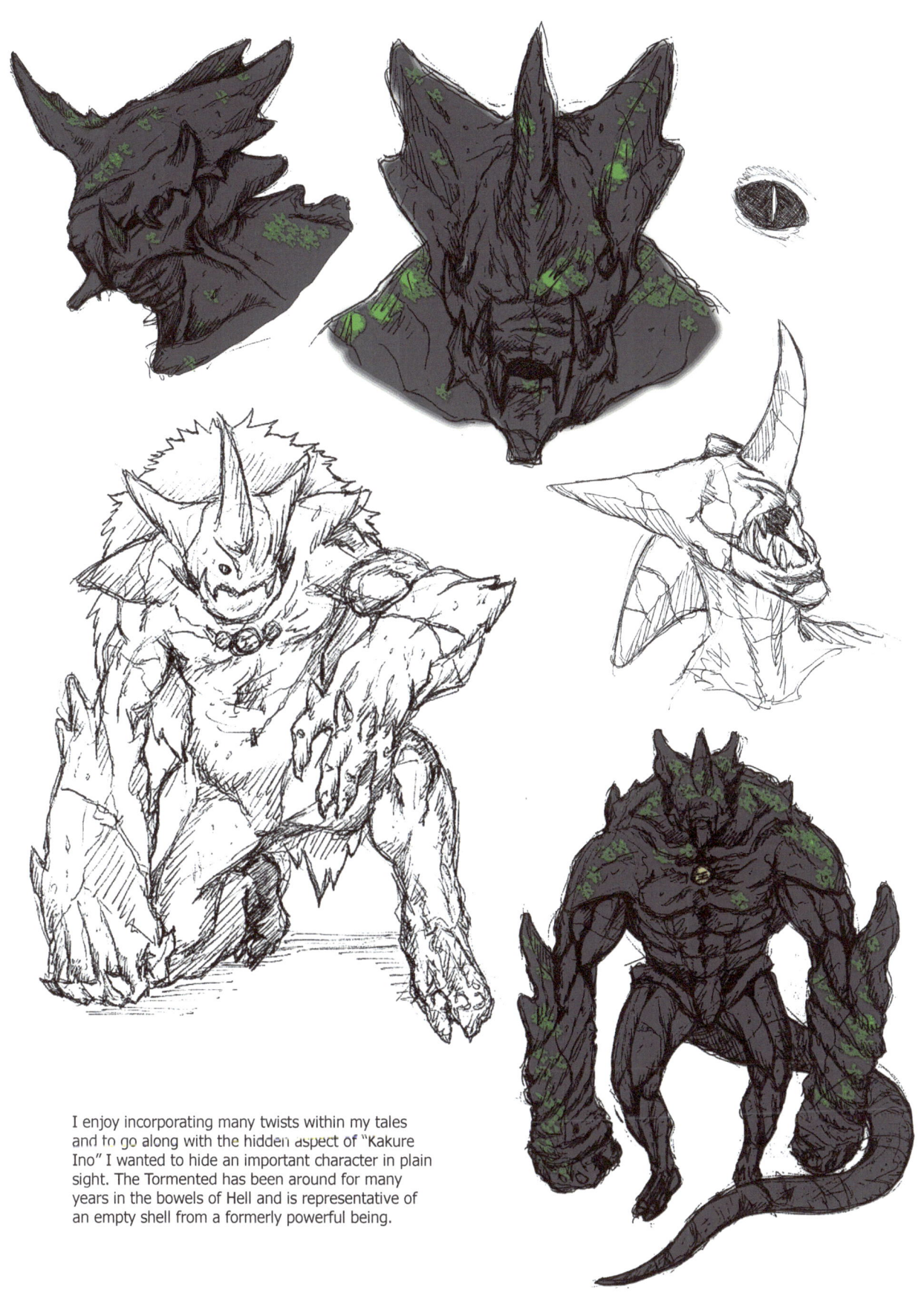

I enjoy incorporating many twists within my tales and to go along with the hidden aspect of "Kakure Ino" I wanted to hide an important character in plain sight. The Tormented has been around for many years in the bowels of Hell and is representative of an empty shell from a formerly powerful being.

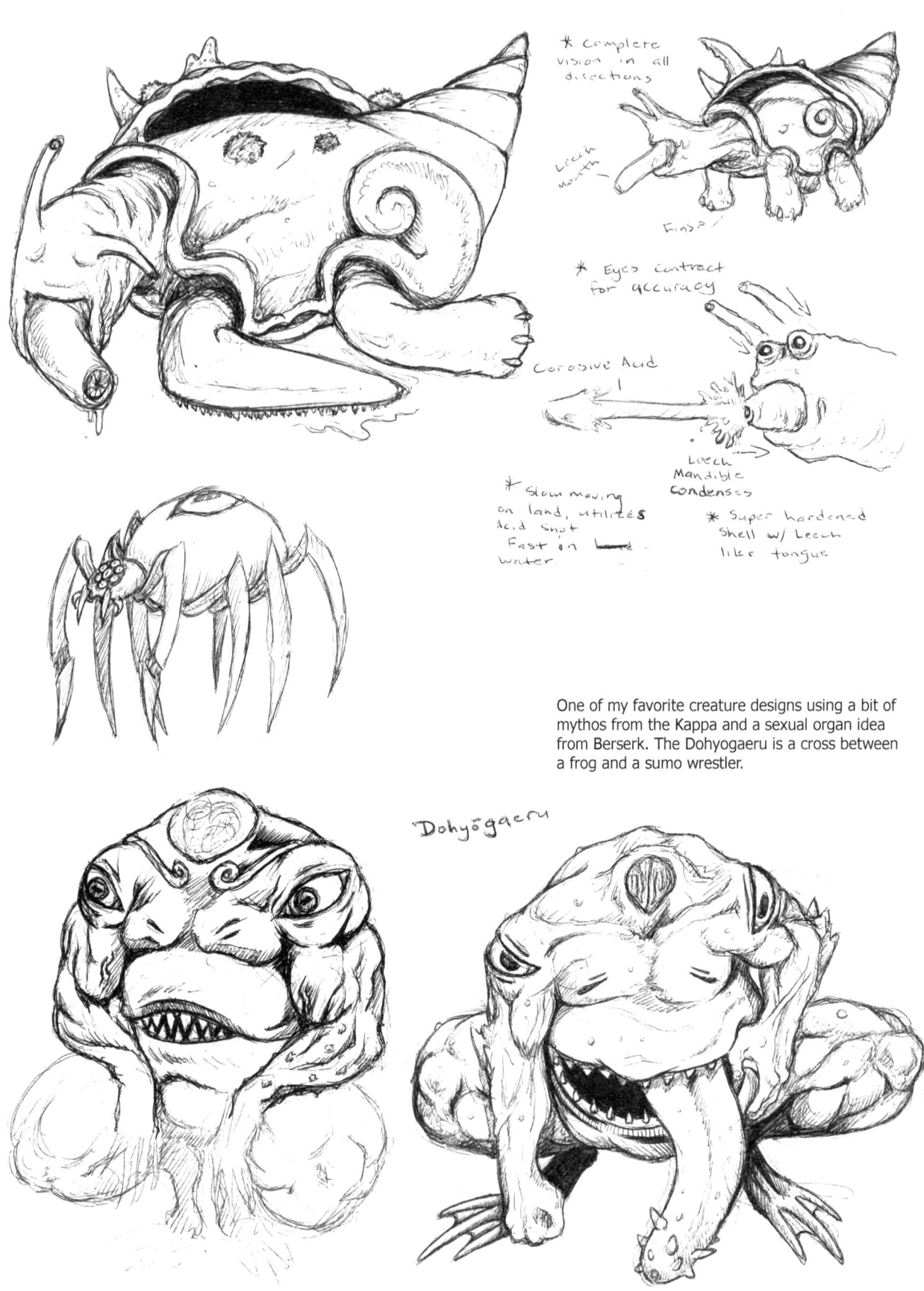

* Complete vision in all directions

Leech mouth

Fins?

* Eyes contract for accuracy

Corrosive Acid

Leech Mandible Condenses

* Slow moving on land, utilizes Acid shot Fast in Water.

* Super hardened Shell w/ Leech like tongue

One of my favorite creature designs using a bit of mythos from the Kappa and a sexual organ idea from Berserk. The Dohyogaeru is a cross between a frog and a sumo wrestler.

Dohyōgaeru

PRIMORDIAL
SERAPH

THE FOUR GUARDIAN BEASTS

In deciding where to take Ino after I had designed her, I chose to implement a concept that is already familiar and twist it into my own thing. The Four Guardian Beasts are entities you've probably heard of in other works; Suzaku, Genbu, Byakko and Seiryuu. The names, abilities, traits and the beasts themselves have been recycled time and time again into different incarnations through out mainstream media.

The beasts govern the four cardinal directions of North (Genbu), South (Suzaku), East (Seiryuu), and West (Byakko) respectively. They resemble beasts in literature and legend, the Suzaku being a Vermillion Bird, Genbu the black tortoise, The Byakko a white tiger and the Seiryuu an azure dragon. In order to create monstrous and epic foes for Ino to overcome, they had to be enormous and extremely powerful, able to eat her in one bite or crush her under foot.

With this simple choice, I was able to practically roll off of this and draw out not only the world, but the overall direction of the story. The number four became a common factor in the overall story. There are 5 protagonists, but four of them are true protagonists and one has a different fate in store. There are four court officials, each with their own motives among other things. In regards to the beasts, I was able to involve the four seasons, in addition to four elements that Ino must encounter en route to face the beasts.

One can imagine how an Oni would fight the Suzaku with its flames, in a scorching heat wave in the southern tip of Japan's Kyushu Island and perched on Mt. Miynouradake with the Suzaku turning the mountain into an active volcano. Or the opposite, Ino must trudge through miles of snow covered land and buried villages of the western Hoshu region to cross a frozen, unstable body of water and meet the Byakko at the heavily forested and snowed in Mishima island. The young oni will face the tremors and earthquakes of the Genbu and the lightning and rainfloods of the Seiryuu as well, all to reach her goal.

Such traits and factors set up for the great task of building the world. I was told once by my good friend Frederick who runs a web manga anthology, to "Build the world first." Although I had planned Ino's story out before meeting him, I myself had forgotten or perhaps not realized how important the world building aspect really was.

On a final note, while the world of Ino practically relies on the Four Guardian Beasts and their ability to affect nature, every other plot aspect trickles down from them. Where the flooded rivers are located, which province or region the Snow Lady Yokai will be fought, How can I get Ino to face a dragon in the sky without something cliche like giving the main character flight. It is all intricately connected to the Guardian Beasts who are the main antagonists of this story, and with that being said, I am hard on Ino because she is my "daughter" and I want her to struggle and grow as a character.

A protagonist must have different struggles with different types of adversaries. Challenge your characters...

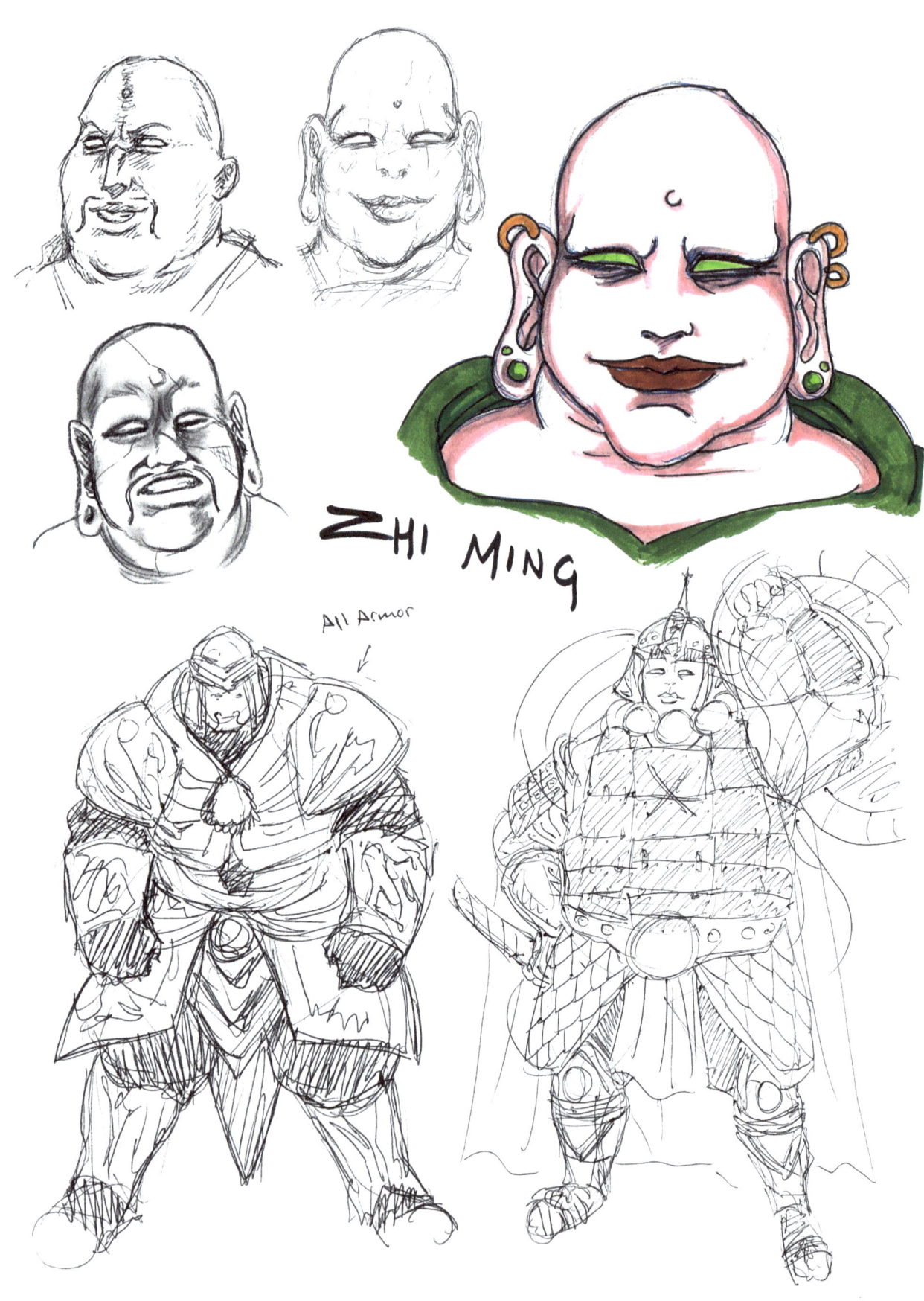

ZHI MING

All Armor

LING GUANG

Leathered Tassets

Golden heeled Leggings

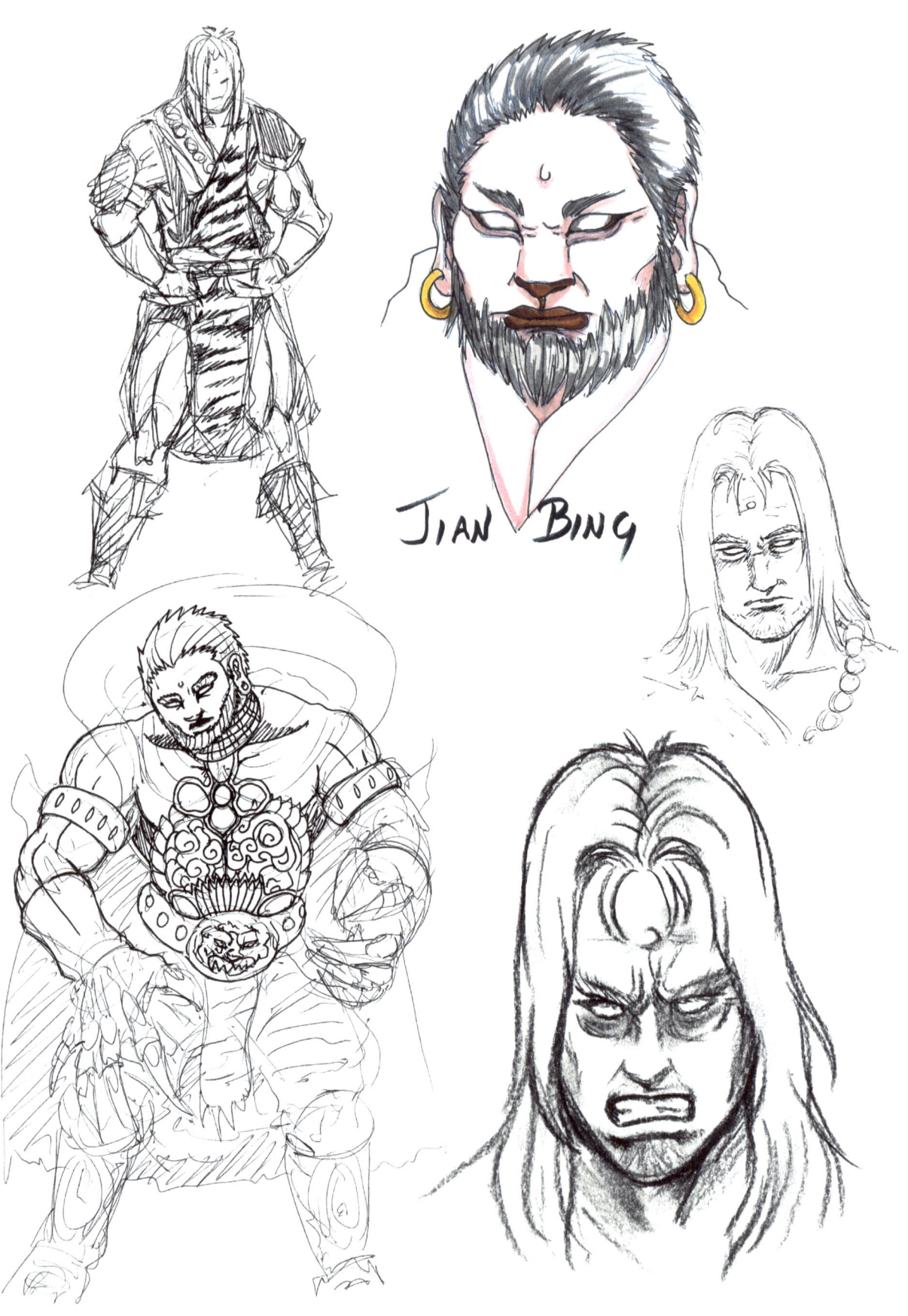

JIAN BING

Golden
Dragon
Pauldron

Large
Golden
Tasset

More
ornate
boots

MengZhang

KNOWING YOUR SUBJECT MATTER

Even in fictuous works, it is a necessity that a creator is familiar with his subject matter. There are several valid reasons that this must be done even in the most vivid of fantasies. Ranging from random tales of silliness to the most straight forward and serious stories, a work has to be immersive and to some degree; believable. It has to make enough sense to retain interest for your reader/viewer. Other reasons include personal interest, although a work in part is done for personal pleasures or the satisfaction of its creator, it must also evenly be so for its consumers, the fans of the creator. Personal interest in the subject matter whether the story is about sci-fi, samurai or crime drama, is what keeps the creator's passion flowing and allows them to continue the work from beginning to end without loss of motivation or inspiration. They are continually involved in the lifestyle or study of the subject and have a burning desire to share their interests with like minds.

Believability ranges from fantasy to realism, however, a certain degree of that believablity is required to hook and catch readers when committing to a continuing story line or even in design works. Concepts must retain some transparency in their design so that there is form and a truth to it even if you completely made it up. The thing itself is "real" in the mind of the reader/viewer and has substance and can become a valid topic of conversation without much confusion or lack of clarity. How does Ino's Kanabo attach to her back? Why can Shuten Doji speak human language and the other oni cannot? Is Gyuki's coat made of actual flame or is it really just fur? These small things often creep into the minds of the reader and

while it need not be answered blatantly, it helps to have function and understanding as well as attention to detail. The reason for this is because people love to challenge what they do not understand. Forums are made daily on who, what, where, and why in regards to a design or concept where fans constantly discuss these things without the creator even being aware of them. While it may not hurt your pockets to pay mind to the forums, what hurts in the long run may be the actual critics or reviewers who have a voice and might feel the need to nitpick. Cover your ass.

As a Japanese history buff myself, I have taken much interest in the Sengoku (feudal) Era of Japan as well as the Heian Period in which Ino's tale takes place. The Taira regime and the Genji Rebellion of the Minamoto clan plays a small role in the story with the inclusion of Yoshitsune's character. I also own a shinken (a live katana), which I take apart and clean regularly. In regards to samurai manga or story telling, if a warrior needed to clean his sword, I can personally say I am familiar with the process and know the materials neeeded if I ever has to put pencil to paper. While the same can be done watching a video online, what matters here is the research and understanding of your subject matter.

Other loose forms of research include watching movies and playing video games, reading up on your subject matter and the like. Those who share those interests will love your work with as much ferver and passion as you do and might even defend your work from naysayers.

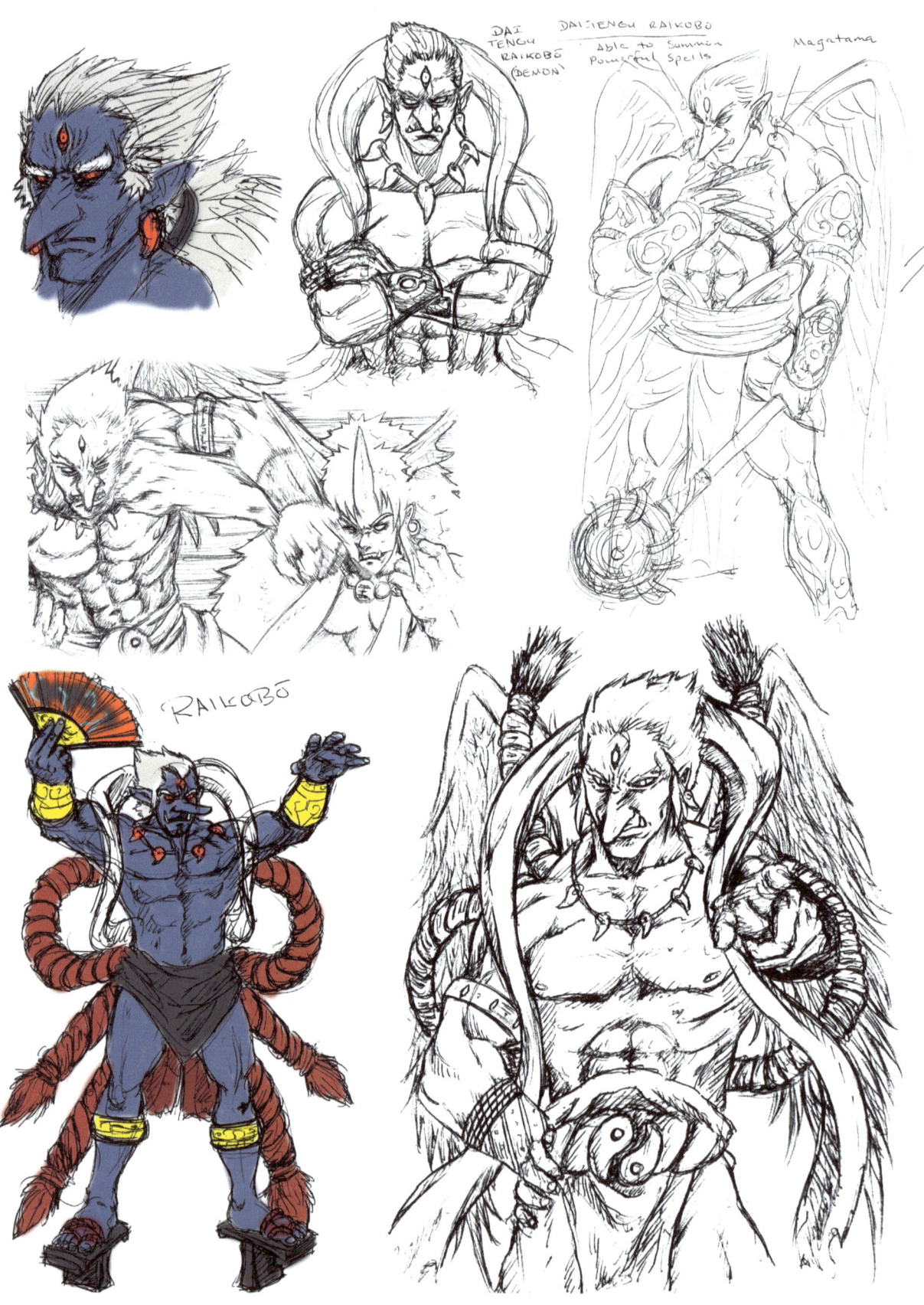

DAI
TENGU
RAIKOBŌ
(DEMON)

DAITENGU RAIKOBŌ
Able to summon Powerful Spells

Magatama

RAIKOBŌ

AMANO-JAKU
INO

UAIROCANA
INO

FULL
ONI
INO

NIO

Ino's Nio Form

The Nio Guardians are the twin defenders of Buddhist principles. Ironically Nio Ino and Oni are anagrams and fit the purpose of this transformation.

I had originally intended for this form to be berserk and demonic, but since Ino is a combination of her father, mother and the Four Guardian Beasts, I decided to go the noble route.

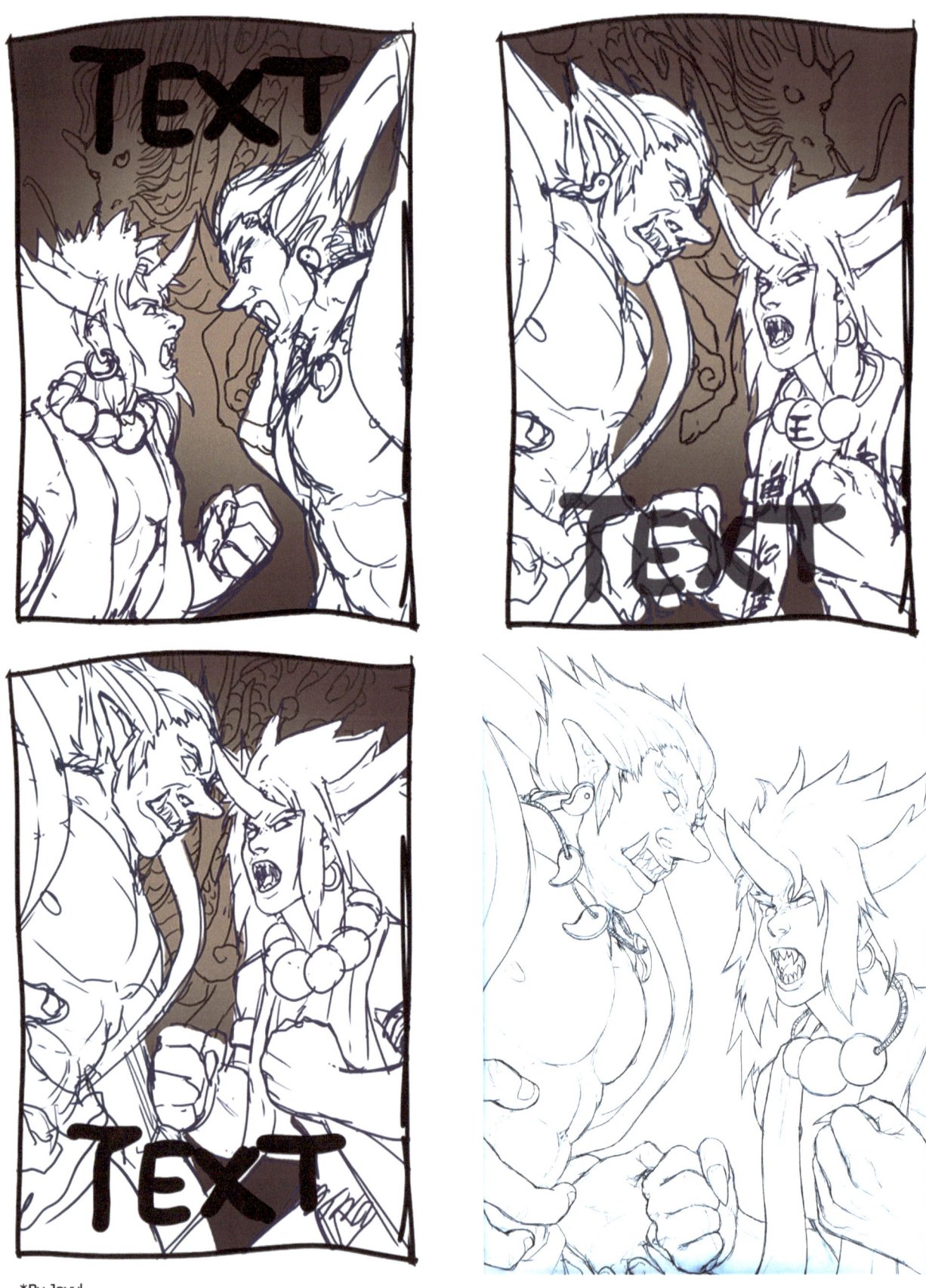

THE *Beauty Marks* COLLECTION

UPCOMING
BOOK BY

Yakusan

In a quest to perfect the art of the female figure, the perfect example had to be used; the living muse! Beauty Marks is the study codex of the woman in her purest form and the results of training thereafter.

COMING SPRING
2017

www.ingramcontent.com/pod-product-compliance
Lightning Source LLC
Chambersburg PA
CBHW042135120726

47911CB00022B/63